The Sky's the Limit!

By Alexandra Reid
Designed & Illustrated by
John & Anthony Gentile,
Louis Henry Mitchell and Joe Schettino

 HarperFestival®
A Division of HarperCollinsPublishers

Look for these other Sky Dancers® books:

April Blossom's Wedding

Lacey's Dancing Shoes

Moon Shimmer's Birthday Party

Sea Starr's Day at the Beach

Hollyberry's Christmas Surprise
A Sky Dancers® Pop-Up Book

Sky-High Hopes
Coloring & Puzzle Book

No Place But Up!
Coloring & Puzzle Book

The Sky's the Limit!

It was the first day of classes at the High Hope Dance Academy, which had just been built on top of Mount High Hope. Jade, Camille, Angelica, Breeze, and Slam could not wait for classes to begin, so they got to the Academy early that day.

When they walked into the classroom, a beautiful woman was standing at the barre. There were two dogs sitting at her feet.

"Welcome, students," she said. "I am Dame Skyla, your teacher and the founder of the Academy. And these are my constant companions, Whirl and Twirl. Now why don't you tell me a little about yourselves and what your dance experience has been."

Jade stepped forward. "I've been studying classical ballet since I was three. The only other thing I like almost as much as ballet is science." She pirouetted gracefully.

"I'm Native American," said Breeze. "And I dance the steps that my grandfather and his grandfather before him passed on to my tribe."

"Modern dance is what I like," said Camille. "And the less traditional, the better!"

"I'm with you," said Slam. He spun around on his heels to show his favorite hip-hop move.

"And I've got the fastest feet in the West," said Angelica, doing a quick square-dance step. "Country, rock, western—I love those rhythms! They make my feet get up and spin around, and the rest of me just follows!"

"Thank you, students," said Dame Skyla. "Different as your dance styles are, you are all joined by your love of dancing. Now let us begin. You have much to learn and I have much to teach!"

Day after day, the five dancers practiced as hard as they could. Then one day Dame Skyla told them they were ready to perform in front of the entire school. "Hooray!" they shouted.

On the night of the performance, the five dancers stood onstage at the Dance Hall while Dame Skyla spoke to the audience. "These are the most gifted students I have ever had," she said. "Their dancing is not just a talent, but a gift to you all. So please welcome Jade, Camille, Angelica, Breeze, and Slam!" The audience clapped loudly.

First each of the five dancers danced alone. Then they joined one another in a beautiful dance that blended their different styles.

When they were finished, the audience gave them a standing ovation.

But when the dancers went backstage to see Dame Skyla, she was gone!

"I made a mistake in my solo," said Slam. "Do you think she's mad?"

"No, I'm sure she's not," said Angelica. "She always tells us mistakes are part of learning."

"Shh!" said Jade. "Do you hear something? It sounds like music, but it's very far away."

"Let's find it," said Breeze. "Maybe that's where Dame Skyla is."

So the dancers followed the faraway music through the halls of the Dance Academy.

The music led the dancers right to the foot of a marble staircase. At the top of the staircase were huge doors.

"The music is coming from behind those doors," said Angelica. "And look, there are Whirl and Twirl. Dame Skyla must be inside."

"Those doors are shaped like wings!" said Breeze.

"They're not shaped like wings," said Camille, her eyes widening in astonishment. "They are wings! And they're opening to let us in."

"They must be activated by some hidden sensor," said Jade.

"What are we waiting for?" said Slam. "Let's go!"

The dancers walked up the steps and through the fluttering wing doors into the most wonderful room they had ever seen. It was two or three times taller than a regular room, and there was a huge stained-glass window showing a crystal-shaped stone with wings.

The walls were lined with hundreds of music boxes of all shapes and sizes and colors and designs, and all the music boxes were playing the music the dancers had been following.

In the middle of the room was a single crystal music box on a pedestal. Next to the pedestal stood Dame Skyla.

"Welcome," Dame Skyla said. "I have been expecting you."

"Why did you leave, Dame Skyla?" asked Slam. "Didn't you like our dancing?"

"Of course I liked it. You were wonderful! So wonderful, in fact, that you are ready to learn the truth. Behold, I am not really Dame Skyla, but Queen Skyla, Queen of the Wingdom and ruler of the Sky Realm." As she spoke, she opened shimmery wings and flew up into the air. The dancers could not believe their eyes.

"The Sky Realm is a special place where the Sky Dancers live," continued Queen Skyla. "The Sky Dancers are peaceful, but the evil Sky Clone wants to steal their gift of flight. We need help, and that is why I came here. I opened the Dance Academy to find the best dancers to take back with me to the Sky Realm and protect it. You are those dancers."

"But how can dancing protect anything?" asked Slam.

"You have not yet learned that dancing can give you special powers. But before I teach you how to find those powers, you must see what Sky Clone has done to the Wingdom." Queen Skyla glided down and held out her wing. The wing began to glow, and looking in it the dancers saw a beautiful city high in the clouds.

"That is the Wingdom," explained Queen Skyla. "And those are the Sky Dancers flying about the clouds."

Next they saw a huge dark shadow being cast into a palace room. In the room was the winged stone shown in the stained-glass window.

"That is Sky Clone, our deadly enemy. He is stealing the Sky Swirl Stone, which gives us the ability to fly. Without the stone, the Sky Dancers and all of the Wingdom would perish."

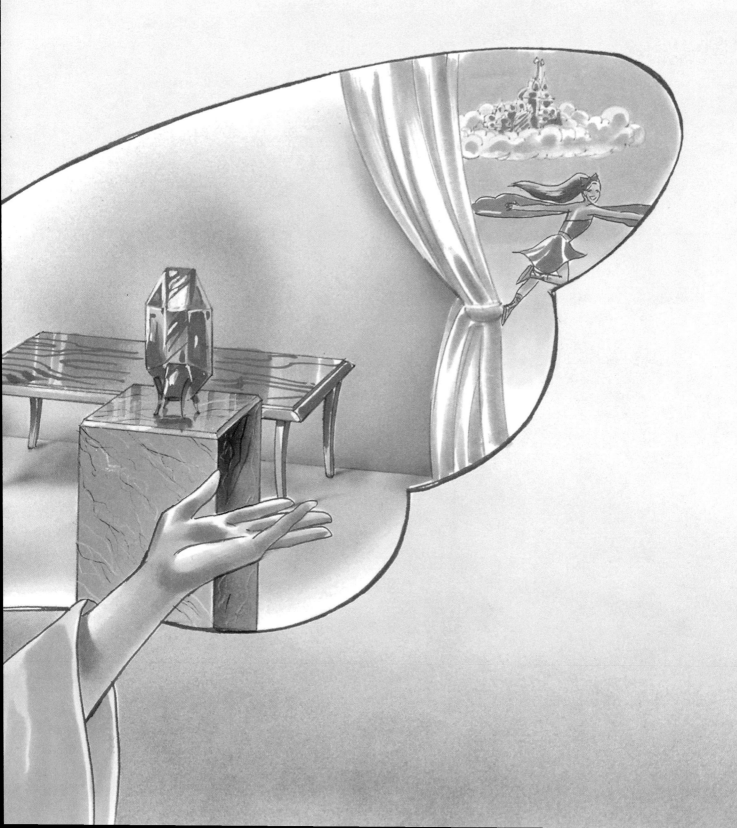

The dancers watched as Sky Clone grabbed the Sky Swirl Stone. Jade covered her eyes.

"You must watch to understand," said Queen Skyla. "See, my husband, King Skyler, came to the rescue."

King Skyler grabbed the Sky Swirl Stone away from Sky Clone. He placed the Stone back on its pedestal and then held Sky Clone tightly. Whirling rapidly around, he threw Sky Clone out of the palace. Then he sank down to the ground.

"That is called a death spin," said Queen Skyla sadly. "My husband saved the Stone and the Wingdom, but in so doing, he was lost forever. As his power faded, he called me to his side and gave me five feathers from his wing. He told me one day I would need them to save the Wingdom from Sky Clone."

Next the Queen showed the five dancers a dark and frightening place that was part castle, part dungeon, and part kaleidoscope. "Sky Clone fell many miles below the Wingdom to a place called the Netherworld. In the fall, he lost his wings and became a monstrous creature, half man and half wind. Now all he wants is to destroy all the Sky Dancers."

"Sky Clone lives in the Netherworld attended by his three henchmen, Snarl, Jumble, and Muddle, and the Terrornadoes and the Horrorcanes. They are ugly creatures made of wind and hate who destroy everything in their path. Even as we speak Sky Clone is preparing to unleash his Terrornadoes on the Wingdom. The tune these music boxes play tells me this."

"What can we do to help, Queen Skyla?" Angelica asked.
"We'll do anything to protect the Wingdom," said Slam.
"Your dancing will give you the power to save my world. Will you agree to become Sky Dancers and battle Sky Clone?"
"Of course we will!" the five dancers cried.

Queen Skyla took out five feathers from her dress. "These are the Rite-of-Flight feathers King Skyler gave to me. They will transform you into Sky Dancers. Now, repeat after me: If it is to be, it's up to me."

The dancers together chanted, "If it is to be, it's up to me" as the Queen touched the feathers against each of their foreheads. Then she pinned the feathers to the dancers.

There was a flash of light, and the dancers felt themselves spinning around and around.

"Now *this* is dancing!" said Breeze.

"We're getting smaller," said Jade. "Or the room is getting larger."

"We are getting smaller," said Queen Skyla. "We have to enter the Sky Realm through this music box. It is a doorway to my world."

Queen Skyla opened the top of the crystal music box and flew in. The dancers were drawn in after her on a golden beam of light.

The dancers found themselves swirling through clouds and mist. Then, all of a sudden, they tumbled into light.

"We can fly!" shouted Angelica. "We've got wings! We can do anything!"

"This is more fun than dancing!" said Slam, doing a somersault in the air.

"This is just not possible," said Jade.

"Come, Sky Dancers, let me show you the Sky Realm," said Queen Skyla.

The Sky Dancers flew behind the Queen, and she led them down through the clouds.

"The Etherians live in these clouds," said Queen Skyla. "They are so light they can float in the cloud currents. If you look closely, you may see one."

Soon the clouds parted, revealing a rich green forest high on top of a mountain.

"That is Skyridian," continued the Queen. "The Skyridiums live there, spending their days dancing and flying around their Harp of Might."

"I see them!" cried Camille as they flew over a clearing in the trees.

"I thought only Sky Dancers lived in the Sky Realm," said Breeze.

"Oh, no," said Queen Skyla. "Sky Dancers live in the Wingdom, but there are many other cities in the Sky Realm and many different races. But we all live together in peace. Living in those blue clouds, for example, are the Azurians. They are Sky Swimmers. Clouds are to them what water on earth is to fish."

"And finally," Queen Skyla said as she led the Sky Dancers down to a cloud bank of gigantic flowers, "there is the city of Sky Hive. The Sky Hivers live in those flowers."

"Where is the Wingdom?" asked Camille.

"Here," said Queen Skyla, leading them down toward a shimmering, shining city. "And there is the Palace of High Hope, my home."

They glided into a the great hall of a towering castle. "This is the High Court, where the Sky Swirl Stone used to be."

"Where is the stone now?" asked Jade.

Queen Skyla lifted her hand. On one finger was a glittering, dazzling stone. "Right here," she said. "It's always with me, as is the memory of King Skylar. One day I hope . . . Why, what is it, Twirl?"

Twirl was growling at the doors that led out to the High Court terrace. Whirl began barking.

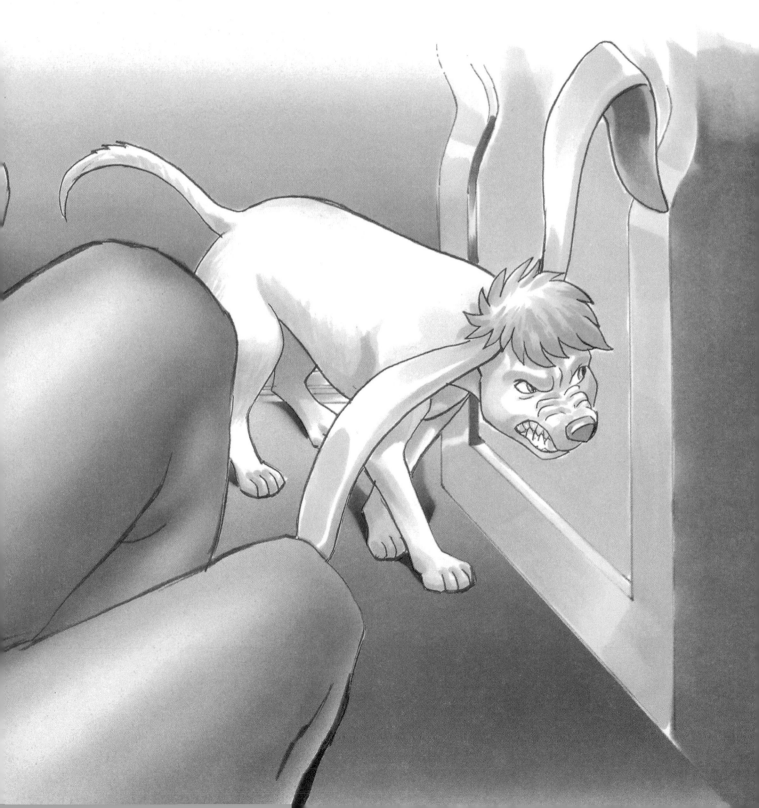

Everyone glided out to the terrace. A terrible whirling monster was heading straight at them.

"It's one of Sky Clone's Terrornadoes!" cried Camille.

"I'll take care of it," said Slam. "Don't worry." He flew into a dizzying series of somersaults, but instead of destroying the Terrornado, he flew right through it!

Next Breeze flew at the monster, but he was quickly thrown aside by the force of the whirling winds. Shaken, Slam and Breeze flew back to the others.

"Now what?" asked Slam.

"Let's all work together," said Jade.

"Good idea!" said Angelica. "Let's press our wings to one another."

The Sky Dancers formed a line and started flying at the Terrornado. Almost immediately the Terrornado spun away and flew down toward the Netherworld.

"Hooray!" the Sky Dancers shouted. "We did it, Queen Skyla!"

But the Queen said sadly, "No, Sky Dancers, the Terrornado just went to warn Sky Clone about you. Oh, there is so little time and so much you need to know if we are to save the Sky Realm."

"Then let's begin right now!" said Breeze.

Queen Skyla smiled. "You are right. We will begin your lessons now."

First Queen Skyla taught the Sky Dancers how to fly upside down and backward, shoot straight up in the air, and glide gracefully down. She taught them how to stop in midair and how to hover.

"Good, Sky Dancers," Queen Skyla said finally. "But you must learn to do more than fly if you are to defeat Sky Clone. Each of you has special powers deep inside yourself, and only with those powers can you save the Sky Realm. You must discover them for yourself, but I can help you."

"Slam," she said, "let's begin with you." She stretched out her hands, and golden beams of light shot from her wingtips and surrounded Slam.

"I feel incredible!" Slam exclaimed. He started breakdancing and then did a somersault in the air.

When he landed he pointed his hands at Queen Skyla, who began to float upward with Whirl and Twirl at her side.

"Excellent, Slam," she said, looking down at him. "You have discovered that your special power is the power of gravity. When you dance, you can move people and objects any way you want."

Next Queen Skyla's golden beams surrounded Camille, who began doing a modern dance. When she stopped, thick white clouds appeared near her hands. She quickly made a small cloud sculpture of a cat.

Whirl and Twirl began barking at the cloud cat. They leapt toward it, yelping with surprise as they passed right through it. The Sky Dancers laughed.

"I guess my special power is to create cloud sculptures," said Camille.

"I wish I could see an instant replay of that," said Slam, still laughing.

"Maybe you can," answered Angelica, "because I have the feeling my special power may have to do with time. Can I go next, Queen Skyla?"

"Of course," she responded.

Angelica started doing cartwheels as the golden beams reached her, and silvery metallic flashes came flying out of her boot heels. When the flashes faded, everything was silent and still.

"Is everyone frozen?" asked Angelica. Nobody said anything. Then Angelica noticed Camille's cloud cat had come back. Immediately everyone unfroze, and Whirl and Twirl chased the cat who disappeared just as it had before.

"Time change is your power," said Queen Skyla. "You can reverse or fast-forward time by a few seconds."

Jade stepped forward. "I'm ready," she said.

As Queen Skyla's golden beams enveloped her, she began pirouetting around the room, and rainbow-colored beams appeared by her feet. But then the bright colors began to fade, and Jade stopped dancing.

"Your power will only work if you believe in it," said Queen Skyla.

"But this is all scientifically impossible," said Jade.

"Don't think about science," encouraged Queen Skyla. "Just believe in yourself and anything can happen."

Jade started dancing again. Soon the rainbow beams appeared, and this time they got brighter and brighter. All of a sudden Jade disappeared.

"Where did she go?" asked Breeze anxiously.

"I'm right here," a voice said at his elbow. Slowly Jade rematerialized.

"My special power is becoming invisible," said Jade. Turning to Queen Skyla she added, "And I do believe now that anything can happen."

Breeze was last to go. As he finished dancing one of his favorite Native American dances, a small cloud drifted over the other Sky Dancers. Rain began pouring down on them.

"Hey, stop it, Breeze! We're getting all wet!" said Slam.

"Sorry!" said Breeze as the cloud disappeared. A warm, gentle wind began to blow, and soon everyone was dry again.

"I guess you're our weatherman," joked Angelica.

"Dancing makes your powers come alive, and the better you dance, the stronger your powers will be," said Queen Skyla.

All of a sudden one of Queen Skyla's servants came flying in. "It's Sky Clone, your Majesty!" he cried. "And there are two Horrorcanes with him!"

"The time has come to defend the Sky Realm," said Queen Skyla, turning to the five Sky Dancers. "What do you say?"

"If it is to be, it's up to me!" they all shouted. Then they flew out to the terrace. Far below they saw Sky Clone riding one Horrorcane while Snarl, Jumble, and Muddle rode the other.

"Let's go get them!" said Angelica. They swooped down toward Sky Clone and the Horrorcanes.

"Look, Sky Clone. It's the Sky Dancers!" shouted Jumble as the five came closer and closer.

"Sky Dancers!" sneered Sky Clone. "Horrorcanes, blow them out of the sky!"

The Horrorcanes whirled quickly toward the Sky Dancers.

"Ready or not, here they come!" shouted Camille.

"I'm going to blast those Horrorcanes with a special lightning bolt," said Breeze. He started dancing furiously, and a lightning bolt zigzagged out of his hands toward a Horrorcane.

The bolt crashed into the Horrorcane, but then bounced off and came streaking back toward the Sky Dancers.

"Duck!" shouted Jade.

The lightning bolt went zinging past, singeing the tips of their wings.

"Now I'm really mad," said Slam, brushing the ashes off his shoulders. "I'm going to use my gravity power and hurl those Horrorcanes right back to the Netherworld."

He somersaulted close to one of the Horrorcanes. But as the gravity beams started shooting from his hands, he found himself being pulled into the the center of the storm cloud.

"I don't think my idea was such a good one after all!" he shouted. In a few seconds he was in the center of the Horrorcane. Every time he tried to break free, Snarl, Jumble, or Muddle pushed him back in.

"I'll destroy you in no time, Sky Dancers," said Sky Clone.

Jade pirouetted and quickly became invisible. "I'm coming, Slam," she said. She snuck up behind Snarl and hurled him to one side. She grabbed Muddle's ankle and threw him far away, and then flung Jumble aside.

Slam flew out of the Horrorcane. "Thanks, Jade, wherever you are," he said. He felt her hand on his shoulder.

"Let's get back to the others," she said.

"The Horrorcanes were too much for me," said Breeze, when they were all back at the High Court.

"Me too," said Slam. "Without Jade, I'd still be spinning around in there."

"We're just not strong enough to stop Sky Clone," said Angelica.

"No!" said Jade. "Alone we're not strong enough, but if we work together we can do anything we want!"

"If it is to be, it's up to me—and all of us!" shouted Slam and Breeze.

"I have a plan," said Jade. "Let's go to the roof and I'll explain."

"Does everyone understand?"Jade asked, when she had finished explaining her plan. The others nodded. "Then let's go!"

Camille quickly made a cloud-castle sculpture, and Breeze and Slam headed for the Horrorcanes. One of the Horrorcanes began chasing Breeze, and the other began chasing Slam. They led the Horrorcanes closer and closer to Camille's cloud castle.

Just as the Horrorcanes were about to capture Breeze and Slam, Camille shouted, "Now!" and Breeze and Slam flew straight up in the air. Angelica hovered on one side of the castle, and Jade hovered on the other.

"Over here, you big bag of wind!" shouted Angelica. "After that Sky Dancer!" shouted Sky Clone, pointing at Angelica. The Horrorcane started closing in on Angelica. On the other side of the cloud castle, the second Horrorcane began whirling toward Jade. They got closer and closer, but Jade and Angelica did not move.

Finally Camille shouted, "Now!" and Jade and Angelica flew up. The Horrorcanes couldn't stop in time. They flew right into the castle and into one another!

The Sky Dancers cheered as the Horrorcanes disintegrated into little puffs of wind. As Sky Clone fell back to the Netherworld, the Sky Dancers heard him shout, "I'll be baaaccckk. . . ."

"Hooray!" Breeze shouted.
"That was fun!" said Camille.
"Let's tell Queen Skyla what happened," said Angelica.
They flew back to the High Court.

"Congratulations, Sky Dancers," said Queen Skyla. "You didn't let me down, and more important, you didn't let yourselves down."

"But Sky Clone will be back," said Jade.

"You won the first battle, and showed Sky Clone he can't win against those who work together as a team," said Queen Skyla. "Let's have a celebration!"

All the inhabitants of the Sky Realm came flying to the Wingdom to join the celebration. For hours they spun and danced with joy and thanked the five Sky Dancers again and again for saving them. Finally they all called for a speech.

Camille pushed Jade forward. "It was your idea that saved us, after all," said Breeze.

"We are so pleased to be able to take a part in helping Queen Skyla and the Sky Realm," Jade began. "But it's not just up to the five of us standing here. All of you must help by believing in goodness and truth and flying up against evil. And most important, you have to believe in yourselves. If it is to be, it's up to me!"

"If it is to be, it's up to me!" shouted everyone, cheering and applauding wildly.

After her speech, Jade returned to the other four Sky Dancers.
"Now what happens?" she asked.
"I feel strange," said Slam.
"Me too," said Camille. "Like I'm being pulled somewhere."

Queen Skyla flew to their side. "You're going back to your world now," she said. "But you'll return here someday—probably sooner than you think."

Then they were whirled away into clouds and mist.

Moments later the five dancers found themelves backstage at the Dance Hall. The audience was still applauding their performance.

"I guess time is different in the Sky Realm," said Jade.

"A lot is different there," said Breeze.

"Luckily we get to go back," said Angelica. "Queen Skyla said so."

"I for one can't wait!" said Camille. "Once you've got wings you can do anything. I miss my wings already."

"In the meantime, though, we can't disappoint our public," said Slam. "Let's go take a bow."

Holding hands, they danced their way onto the stage.